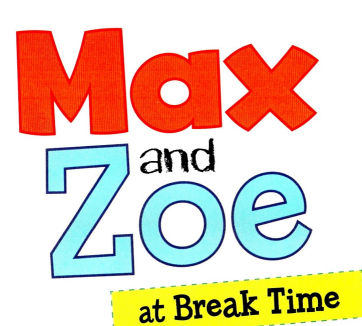

Max and Zoe

at Break Time

by Shelley Swanson Sateren

illustrated by Mary Sullivan

raintree

a Capstone company — publishers for children

Raintree is an imprint of Capstone Global Library Limited, a
company incorporated in England and Wales having its registered
office at 264 Banbury Road, Oxford, OX2 7DY – Registered
company number: 6695582

www.raintree.co.uk
myorders@raintree.co.uk

Designed by Emily Harris
Production by Katy LaVigne
Originated by Capstone Global Library Ltd
Printed and bound in India

ISBN 978 1 4747 9066 6 (hardback)
ISBN 978 1 4747 9072 7 (paperback)

British Library Cataloguing in Publication Data
A full catalogue record for this book is available from
the British Library.

Contents

One day, Max and Zoe's teacher, Ms Young, had a surprise for break time.

"As it's the first snow of the year, I've brought sledges," she said. "Put on your warm clothes!"

The class was very excited

and rushed outside.

"Let's ride together, Max,"

said Zoe. "We'll both push

and go super fast."

"Cool," said Max.

"This will be the best

break time ever!"

Max and Zoe raced towards the snowy hill.

"Max," called Ms Young. She pointed at his shoes. "No boots, no playing in the snow."

"Please?" Max begged.

"Sorry," said Ms Young. "You'll have to stay in the playground."

Zoe frowned. "Not again, Max," she said. "You always forget your boots!"

Max hung his head.

"I'm sorry, Max. But I'm

not going to miss sledging,"

Zoe said and ran away.

Max stood in the

playground by himself while

everyone else went sledging.

"It's not fair," he thought.
"This is the worst break time ever!"

Chapter 2
No shoes

After school, Zoe and Max walked to his flat.

"No more forgetting your boots," Zoe said. "I have a great idea."

They raced to Max's
room. Zoe found felt tips and
a big piece of paper.

Then she made a giant
sign and taped it to Max's
door.

"I'll see that every

morning," said Max.

"That's the plan," said

Zoe. "Then you won't

miss any more sledging

adventures."

The next morning, Max

saw the sign.

"My boots!" he said.

He found one boot under

his bed. The other was under

a big pile of clothes.

On the bus, Zoe said,
"The sign worked! You are
wearing your boots."

"I know," said Max. "It's
so cold today. My feet won't
freeze, and I'll get to sledge!"

"I can't wait," said Zoe.

That afternoon, Ms Young

said, "It's too cold to go

outside for break time today.

We'll play parachute games

in the hall instead."

"I love parachute games," said Zoe.

"Me too," said Max.

At the door to the hall, Ms Young pointed to Max's feet.

"No boots in the hall," she said.

"Oh, no! I left my shoes at home," Max cried.

"Then you'll just have to watch," Ms Young said.

Max had to sit by the wall the whole time.

After break time, the
children headed back to the
classroom.

"You need to start
remembering your stuff,
Max," Zoe said.

"I know," Max said.

Chapter 3
The list

After school, Zoe and Max headed to Max's place again.

"I have another idea," Zoe said. "I need some paper and a pen."

"Here you go," Max said.

"We need to make a list," Zoe said. "Think of everything you need for school. Then write it down."

1. boots
2. shoes
3. hat
4. mittens
5. snow trousers
6. lunch box
7. backpack
8. homework
9. library books

Zoe helped Max search

for everything on the list.

They even found

his missing library

books.

"Wow," said

Max. "I'm ready for school

tomorrow!"

"Just don't forget your backpack," said Zoe.

"No problem," Max said as he hung a new sign on his bedroom door.

The next day at break time, Max and Zoe's class went outside.

Max and Zoe's sledge flew down the snowy hill, again and again.

"This is the fastest we've ever gone!" yelled Zoe.

"This is the BEST break time ever!" yelled Max.

About the author

Shelley Swanson Sateren is the award-winning author of many children's books. She has worked as a children's book editor and in a children's bookshop. Today, as well as writing, Shelley works with primary-school-aged children in various settings. She lives in Minnesota, USA, with her husband and two sons.

About the illustrator

Mary Sullivan has been drawing and writing all her life, which has mostly been spent in Texas, USA. She earned a BFA from the University of Texas in Studio Art.

Glossary

adventures exciting experiences

backpack a large bag that you carry on your back

beg plead with someone to help you

break time at school, a break from lessons to rest and play

forget not remember

parachute a large piece of strong cloth

Discussion questions

1. With Zoe's help, Max learned ways to remember his school things. Talk about a time you forgot something important.

2. Do you prefer having break time inside the hall or outside in the playground? Why?

3. When Max forgot his boots, he didn't get to play in the snow. Do you think that was fair? Why or why not?

Writing prompts

1. Make a list of five items you need to take to school.

2. At break time, Max loves to go sledging and play parachute games. Write a few sentences about what you like to do at break time.

3. Zoe helps Max learn to remember his things. Write a few sentences about a time when a friend has helped you with something.

Make a postbox

There are a lot of things to remember to take to school. Keeping track of school forms can be tricky. Make an IN postbox and an OUT postbox to stay organized.

What you need:

- 2 large cereal boxes, the same size
- light-coloured paper, such as yellow or orange
- dark-coloured felt tips, such as blue or green
- scissors
- glue

What you do:

1. Cut out the top of both cereal boxes.

2. Using glue, cover the outside of the boxes with coloured paper.

3. Lay the boxes on their backs.

4. On the top of one box, write IN with a felt tip. Write OUT on the top of the other box.

5. Take school forms out of your backpack. Put them in the IN box. Your parent will sign them and put them in the OUT box.

6. At night, put the finished forms back into your backpack.

The fun doesn't stop here!

We have lots more Max and Zoe adventures for you to enjoy!

Discover more books and favourite characters at **www.raintree.co.uk**